Tadpoles
Nursery Rhymes

Little Miss
Muffet

and

Little Miss
Mumpet

Notes for adults

TADPOLES NURSERY RHYMES are structured to provide support for newly independent readers. The books may also be used by adults for sharing with young children.

The language of nursery rhymes is often already familiar to an emergent reader, so the opportunity to see these rhymes in print gives a highly supportive early reading experience. The alternative rhymes extend this reading experience further, and encourage children to play with language and try out their own rhymes.

If you are reading this book with a child, here are a few suggestions:

1. Make reading fun! Choose a time to read when you and the child are relaxed and have time to share the story.
2. Recite the nursery rhyme together before you start reading. What might the alternative rhyme be about? Why might the child like it?
3. Encourage the child to reread the rhyme, and to retell it in their own words, using the illustrations to remind them what has happened.
4. Point out together the rhyming words when the whole rhymes are repeated on pages 12 and 22 (developing phonological awareness will help with decoding language) and encourage the child to make up their own alternative rhymes.
5. Give praise! Remember that small mistakes need not always be corrected.

First published in 2008 by
Franklin Watts
338 Euston Road
London NW1 3BH

Franklin Watts Australia
Level 17/207 Kent Street
Sydney NSW 2000

Text (Little Miss Mumpet)
© Mick Gowar 2008
Illustration © Jan Smith 2008

The rights of Mick Gowar to be identified as the author of Little Miss Mumpet and Jan Smith as the illustrator of this Work have been asserted in accordance with the Copyright, Designs and Patents Act, 1988.

ISBN 978 0 7496 8036 7 (hbk)
ISBN 978 0 7496 8042 8 (pbk)

Series Editor: Jackie Hamley
Series Advisor: Dr Hilary Minns
Series Designer: Peter Scoulding

The author and publisher would like to thank Frances Gowar for permission to reproduce the photograph on p. 14.

Printed in China

Franklin Watts is a division of Hachette Children's Books an Hachette Livre UK company.
www.hachettelivre.co.uk

Little Miss
Muffet

Retold by Mick Gowar
Illustrated by Jan Smith

W
FRANKLIN WATTS
LONDON • SYDNEY

Jan Smith

"Little Miss Muffet was one of my favourite nursery rhymes, because as soon as my mum said, '... who sat down beside her...' I knew I was about to get tickled!"

Little Miss Muffet
sat on a tuffet,

eating her curds
and whey.

Along came a spider,
who sat down
beside her,

and frightened
Miss Muffet away!

Little Miss Muffet

Little Miss Muffet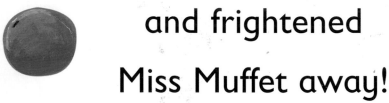

sat on a tuffet,

eating her curds and whey.

Along came a spider,

who sat down beside her,

and frightened

Miss Muffet away!

Can you point to the
rhyming words?

Little Miss Mumpet

by Mick Gowar
Illustrated by Jan Smith

13

Mick Gowar

"This is me in my shed. This is where I write my books. When I'm not writing I like visiting schools to read my books and tell stories to the children."

Little Miss Mumpet
found an old trumpet,

and sat herself
down on the hay.

Along came a spider,
who sat down
beside her,

19

and taught
Miss Mumpet to play!

Little Miss Mumpet

Little Miss Mumpet
found an old trumpet,
and sat herself down on the hay.
Along came a spider,
who sat down beside her,
and taught
Miss Mumpet to play!

Can you point to the
rhyming words?

Puzzle Time!

Which of these instruments do you blow to play?

Answers